When I Am Old with You

Story by ANGELA JOHNSON   Pictures by DAVID SOMAN

Orchard Books
An Imprint of Scholastic Inc.
New York

Text copyright © 1990 by Angela Johnson
Illustrations copyright © 1990 by David Soman

ISBN 978-0-531-07035-2

40 39 38 37 36 35 34 33 32   16 17 18 19 20

Library of Congress Cataloging-in-Publication Data
Johnson, Angela. When I am old with you / by Angela Johnson ; illustrated by David Soman.
p.   cm. "A Richard Jackson book." Summary: A child imagines being old with
Grandaddy and joining him in such activities as playing cards all day, visiting the ocean,
and eating bacon on the porch.
ISBN 0-531-05884-0.   ISBN 0-531-08484-1 (lib. bdg.)
[1. Grandfathers—Fiction.   2. Old age—Fiction.]   I. Soman, David, ill.   II. Title.
PZ7.J629Wh   1990   [E]—dc20   89-70928   CIP   AC

Manufactured in the United States of America.   08
Book design by Mina Greenstein.
The text of this book is set in 18 pt. ITC Caslon 224 Book.
The illustrations are watercolor paintings reproduced in full color.

To my parents, Arthur and Truzetta

A. J.

To my grandma
for a lifetime of love and support

D. S.

When I am old with you, Grandaddy,
I will sit in a big rocking chair beside you
and talk about everything.

An old dog will sit by my feet,
    and I will swat flies all afternoon.

We'll go fishing too, Grandaddy, down by that
old pond with the flat rocks all around.

We can fish beside the pond or take that old canoe out.

We'll eat out of the picnic basket all day and we won't catch any fish…

…but that's all right, Grandaddy.

When I am old with you, Grandaddy, we will
play cards all day underneath that old tree by the road.

We'll drink cool water
from a jug and wave at all
the cars that go by.

We'll play cards till the lightning bugs shine in the trees…

…and we won't mind that we forgot to keep score, Grandaddy.

When I am old with you, Grandaddy, we will open up that old cedar chest and try on all the old clothes that your grandaddy left you.

We can look at the old pictures and try to imagine the people in them.
It might make us cry…
but that's O.K.

In the mornings, Grandaddy, we will cook
bacon for breakfast and that's all.
We can eat it on the porch too.

In the evening we can roast corn on a big fire
and invite everyone we know to come over and
eat it. They'll all dance, play cards, and talk
about everything.

When I am old with you, Grandaddy, we can
take a trip to the ocean.
Have you ever seen the ocean, Grandaddy?

We'll walk on the hot sand and throw rocks at the waves.

We can wear big hats in the afternoon like everyone else...

...and we'll sit in the water when the day gets cool.

When our trip is over we will follow the ocean as far as we can, so we'll never forget it.

When I am old with you, Grandaddy, we will get on the tractor and ride through the fields of grass.

We will see the trees in the distance and remember when this field was a forest.

We won't be sad though.

Grandaddy, when I am old with you we will take long walks
and speak to all the people who walk by us.
We'll know them all, Grandaddy, and they'll know us.

At the end of our walk, when we're tired,
Grandaddy, I will sit in a big rocking chair...
beside you.